A ROOKIE READER®

CITY BIRDS

By Heather MacLeod

Illustrations by Mary "Ching" Walters

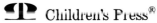 Children's Press®
A Division of Grolier Publishing
New York   London   Hong Kong   Sydney
Danbury, Connecticut

Dedicated to dad and Elissa,
who taught me to notice birds,
and to mom,
who taught me how to read.

Library of Congress Cataloging—in—Publication Data

MacLeod, Heather,
    1958-City Birds / by Heather MacLeod.
      p. cm. — (A Rookie reader)
      ISBN 0-516-02028-5
      1. Birds — Juvenile literature. 2. Urban fauna — Juvenile
literature. [1. Birds. 2. Urban animals.] I. Title. II. Series.

    QL676.2.M335 1995   95-12040
    598—dc20   CIP
                                              AC

Birds in the city, birds in the town,

wherever I go, I see birds all around.

Birds in the park,

Pigeons

birds at a bus stop,

Dove

BUS
STO

birds on a high wire,

Mockingbird

Starling

birds on a rooftop;

Blackbird

birds in my yard,
birds on the sidewalk,

10

Robins

birds all alone,

Hawk

Geese

and birds in a flock,

birds in the water,
birds in the air,

Ducks

14

wherever I look,
I see birds everywhere.

Sparrows

16

Blue Jay

17

Parakeet

18

Birds in cages,

Cockatoo

Parrots

19

birds flying free,

birds in the bushes,

Chickadees

and birds in the trees,

Cardinal

24

birds that are brown,
grey, green, and blue,

Peacocks

birds that are pink
and live in a zoo—

Flamingos

27

All through the city,
all through the town,

wherever I look,
there are birds all around!

Names of City Birds

Blackbird
Blue Jay
Cardinal
Chickadee
Cockatoo
Duck
Flamingo
Goose
Gull
Hawk

Mockingbird
Parakeet
Parrot
Peacock

Pigeon
Robin
Sparrow
Starling

About the Author

Heather MacLeod is a former school librarian and third grade teacher. She got jealous of how much fun her students had writing stories, so she started writing her own. She lives in the city of Oakland, in California. She likes to watch birds, and so does her cat China.

About the Artist

Mary "Ching" Walters has been an artist and designer for more than twenty years. The animals and scenes she draws have appeared on greeting cards, postage stamps, and in children's books. Besides being an artist, Ms. Walters is a licensed pilot, certified scuba diver, and English horseback riding instructor. She lives in Pensacola, Florida, with her husband and dog "Sandy."